© 1993 Geddes & Grosset Ltd
Published by Geddes & Grosset Ltd,
New Lanark, Scotland.

ISBN 1 85534 580 3

Printed and bound in Italy.

The Emperor's New Clothes

Retold by Judy Hamilton
Illustrated by Lindsay Duff

Tarantula Books

A long time ago in a country far away, there once ruled an emperor. The emperor was neither bad nor cruel, but he was very vain. He loved to parade in front of his people magnificently dressed in regal robes, at the head of grand processions.

He loved the admiration of his subjects. In order to look his best, the emperor would spend a lot of his time and a lot of his country's money having manicures and beauty treatments, and most of all, having clothes made. The more exotic the better.

The emperor had wardrobes bursting with silk shirts, velvet and fur capes and jewelled waistcoats.

All the tailors in the country vied with each other to be allowed to make something for the emperor.

One day however, two men arrived at the palace with mischief in mind. They told the guards that they were tailors, and asked for an audience with the emperor. The emperor, naturally, agreed to see them. What they had to say amazed him.

"Your majesty," they told him, "we wish to make you robes of the most special cloth. We weave the cloth ourselves on our own looms, and it has magic powers. A wise person will be able to see the cloth is magnificent, but a fool will see nothing. We have chosen you to be the first to wear this cloth, for you are the wisest and most elegant man in the land."

The wisest and most elegant man!

The emperor, of course, was delighted. He gave the men a bag of gold and told them to start work at once.

The very next day the two rascals set up their looms in a room in the royal palace. They gave orders for the finest golden and silver threads and the most expensive spun silk to be sent to them. But they didn't use this thread. Instead, they packed it all away in sacks to sell for a good price at the market.

They left the looms empty of thread, and instead of weaving, they made themselves comfortable and slept the rest of the day away. They stayed until late that evening. When darkness had fallen, they left.

As they made their way out of the palace gates they told the guards at the gates that the magic cloth was now half-made.

The next day, the two rascals returned and pretended to work on the looms once more.

The emperor was full of curiosity as to what the magic cloth would look like, but he had promised the men that he would not watch them while they were working, or see the cloth before it was finished. Unable to contain his curiosity, he sent his trusted manservant to visit the tailors at their work! The manservant knew about the magic cloth and knew that it was invisible to fools, but he was sure that he was wise enough to see it. He marched up to the workroom, opened the door and went in. Imagine his surprise when he saw the two men sitting working at looms that appeared to be completely empty!

The manservant was most distressed.

"I cannot see this magic cloth!" he thought. "But how can I go back to the emperor and admit it? I will lose my job!"

He stared hard at one of the looms, trying to see the magic cloth, but still he saw nothing there. He decided that he would have to pretend.

"What do you think of our cloth?" one of the men asked, with a wicked gleam in his eye.

"Amazing! Beautiful!" the manservant replied. "But how can I describe such beautiful cloth to the emperor?"

The rascal grinned. "Describe it in this way," he told the manservant, and went on to give him a long description of the exotic design of the cloth.

The emperor was even more excited after he had heard his manservant tell him about the cloth. He could hardly wait for it to be finished. Finally one of the tailors came to tell him that they had completed the weaving and that they would like the emperor to see the cloth before they made it into robes for him.

Just as his manservant had done, he went into the workroom and stared at the empty looms in dismay.

" I cannot see this magic cloth!" he thought. "But I must not let my people know that I am a fool. They would hate to have an ass for an emperor!"

Just as his manservant had done, the emperor decided to pretend that he could see the cloth.

"This cloth is the most beautiful material I have ever seen!" he said to the two rascals. They grinned with delight.

The emperor set about organising a special royal procession, and ordered the tailors to set to work making the cloth into robes.

"It will be a great day when I wear these robes for the first time," he declared.

Word had spread about the emperor's new clothes and the magic cloth. Throughout the land people were saying to themselves:

"I am no fool, I will see these wonderful robes!"

The two rascals worked day and night, pretending to sew. They snipped in the air with scissors as if they were cutting cloth, and moved needles up and down as if they were stitching. They appeared to be very busy. In fact, of course, they were doing nothing at all.

On the morning of the great procession the two men went before the emperor and his courtiers. They held up their hands as if they were holding up clothes for the people of the court to see.

"Our great work is complete your majesty!" they announced. "We hope you are satisfied!"

The emperor's courtiers of course, could see nothing at all. But just as the emperor and his manservant had done, they pretended. They gasped with delight, and exclaimed out loud that the clothes were the most beautiful that they had ever seen.

The emperor was delighted. "You are the most skilful of tailors," he told the men. "I shall reward you handsomely for this! Now we must prepare for the great procession!"

The two men went with the emperor to his chambers. They helped him to undress and pretended to dress him in his new robes.

Trying very hard not to shiver with the cold, the emperor stared into the mirror. He felt sure that if he looked hard enough, he would see the magic robes. But however hard he looked all he could see was his own plump, pink body.

The rascally tailors were enjoying this. "Don't you think, your majesty, that the cut of the robe is perfection itself?" they said.

"Oh yes," said the emperor, "It is quite the finest outfit I have ever worn."

But, secretly, he wished that he was clever enough to see the clothes.

Shortly afterwards, the great procession started off through the streets of the capital, with the emperor and his guards in front. The whole city had been prepared for this great occasion and everybody had come to see the emperor and his new magic robes.

As the emperor slowly passed by, waving to the crowd, everyone thought the same thing.

"If I cannot see the clothes, then I must be a fool!"

And just as the emperor and the manservant and his courtiers had done, they all decided to pretend. Nobody wanted to appear a fool.

"Look at the colours in these robes! Look at the elegant cut of the cloak!" they exclaimed.

The emperor's chest swelled with pride as he heard these remarks. It was so nice to be admired!

The procession moved slowly on its way, and all along the route people politely exclaimed about the magnificent way in which the emperor was dressed.

Then the procession passed by a little boy who had been standing with his mother, waiting to catch a glimpse of the emperor. This little boy had not been told about the magic robes, and he had the courage to say exactly what he was thinking. He took one look at the emperor and burst out laughing.

"The emperor has no clothes on! He looks funny!" he shouted.

All around, people heard him and began to whisper.

"The little boy is right! The emperor is naked!"

The little boy had given them the courage to tell the truth.

The emperor had heard the little boy as well, and was now listening to the mutterings of the crowd. So he was naked after all! Blushing bright pink with embarrassment, he realised what had happened. He was a fool! He had believed the two rascals.

The two wily tailors had made fools of everybody!

Somewhere, safely far away, they were laughing at the success of their trick, and discussing how to spend the fortune that they had made.

Meanwhile the emperor had to walk back to the palace with nothing on apart from his crown. He was cold and ashamed, but much, much wiser.

Never again would he let his vanity stop him from using his common sense.